Library of Congress Cataloging-in-Publication Data

Doney, Meryl, 1942–
    The very worried sparrow / Meryl Doney ; illustrated by Gaby Hansen.
        p. cm.
    Summary: A worried little sparrow learns about God our Father,
who loves and cares for us all.
    ISBN 0-8198-8038-8
    [1. Trust in God—Fiction. 2. Sparrows—Fiction. 3. Worry—Fiction.]
I. Hansen, Gaby, ill. II. Title.
    PZ7.D7165Ve 2008
    [E]—dc22
                                2007025550

Original edition published in English under the title
The Very Worried Sparrow by Lion Hudson plc, Oxford, England.

Text copyright © 2006, Meryl Doney

Illustrations copyright © 2006, Gaby Hansen

Original edition copyright © 2006, Lion Hudson plc

To Micah and the next
generation   M.D.

To my very best friend
Shannon with love   G.H.

"P" and PAULINE are registered trademarks of the Daughters of St. Paul.

First North American edition, 2008

Published by Pauline Books & Media, 50 Saint Pauls Avenue,
Boston, MA 02130-3491. www.pauline.org.

Printed in China.

Pauline Books & Media is the publishing house of the Daughters of St. Paul, an international
congregation of women religious serving the Church with the communications media.

1 2 3 4 5 6 7 8 9   11 10 09 08

Meryl
Doney

ILLUSTRATED BY
Gaby
Hansen

The Very Worried Sparrow

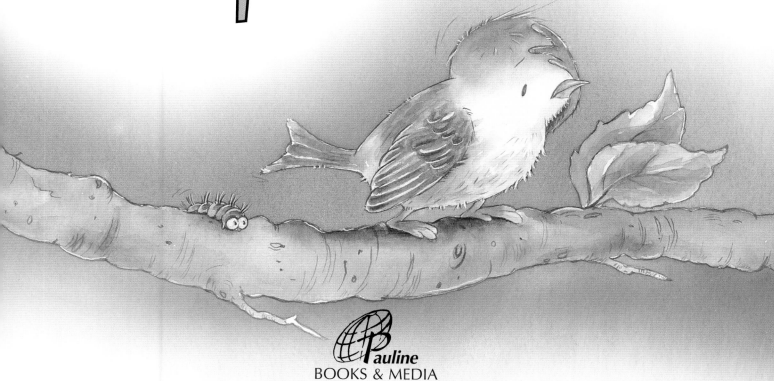

Pauline
BOOKS & MEDIA

There was once a Very Worried Sparrow. All the other baby birds looked up at the bright blue sky and sang, "Cheep, cheep! Cheep, cheep!"

But not the Very Worried Sparrow. "Meep, meep," he said in a very little voice.

The first thing he worried about was food.

"Oh dear!" he thought. "I'm so hungry.
Whatever am I going to eat?"

Suddenly, there was Mother with a fat,
juicy caterpillar for each baby bird.

One day, Father gathered the little
sparrows around him.

"I think it is time you
learned to fly," he said.
"Open your wings and flap."

"Wheeeeeee, this is lovely,"
called the sparrows.

"Meep, meep," said the Very Worried Sparrow.

"I don't dare."

He was so scared he lost his
balance, toppled off the branch...
flipped... and flapped... and flew!

When the sun went down, Father Sparrow
gathered his family together,
warm and snug in the nest.

He told them wonderful stories of long ago and
far away:

of God our Father, who made the world
and everything in it;

of how the day begins, and where the
wind comes from, and all the little things that every
creature knows.

The young birds listened with bright eyes.

But the Very Worried Sparrow peered
out into the darkness. "Meep," he said.
"Oh, dear!"

When summer came, the Very Worried Sparrow
felt just a little braver. He set off with his
brothers and sisters to look for seeds in the field.
    SWOOSH!

The terrible sparrowhawk came diving down. The Very Worried Sparrow closed his eyes tight and waited, too scared to move.

But when he opened them, he saw the sparrowhawk flying away.

"Meep, meep," said the Very Worried Sparrow. "I'm going home!" And he flew to the nest as fast as he could.

The autumn winds blew
and the trees shed their
leaves. Then the snow
fell, covering the ground in
a soft layer of sparkling white.
The sparrows thought it was wonderful.

The Very Worried Sparrow peered about him. "The
snow has covered up all the food," he said. "And where
will we find water to drink?"

But each morning, children scattered seeds
on the path and broke the ice that glazed the
pond. The sparrows had plenty to eat and drink
all through the winter.

Spring came and the sparrows twittered with excitement.

"It's nesting time," they said.

They swooped and sang with all the other sparrows.

Soon pairs of birds were darting away, looking for safe places to build their nests.

"Meep, meep," said the Very Worried Sparrow,
his head drooping. "I'm all alone."

The branch bounced as a little sparrow fluttered closer.

"Cheep," she said shyly.

"Meep, meep," said the Very Worried Sparrow.
"Will you be my friend?"

"Oh yes!" she said happily.

"I know a good place for a nest," she said. "Come and see."
Together they flew to a lovely apple tree.

"Meep, meep," said the Very Worried Sparrow. "It's lovely. But **I** expect other birds have found it already."

"It's a safe place just for us," chirruped his mate. "Come on!"

Before long, the shy
sparrow was sitting in the nest. Under
her warm feathers were four speckled eggs.

"Meep, meep," said the Very Worried Sparrow.

"Soon I'll have a family to worry about."

Far below, in the grass, a cat was prowling.

High above, a sparrowhawk

drifted on the wind.

The Very Worried Sparrow was
looking very, very... worried!
"Roo coo. What's the matter?" asked a gentle voice.
It was the turtledove with soft white feathers.

"I'm so worried," wept the sparrow.

"Roo coo," said the dove.

"Don't you know about God our Father, who made us all and who cares about every sparrow?"

"Meep, meep," said the Very Worried Sparrow.

"I was so worried, I didn't listen."

So, as the sun went down, the dove gathered all the birds around her, and told the stories of long ago and far away:

of God our Father, who made the world and everything in it;

of how the day begins, and where the wind comes from, and all the little things that every creature knows.

She spoke of the seasons and the years, of how things grow and new life comes. She told how God our Father knows each creature and its time on the earth.

The next day, the whole world sparkled in the morning light.

"Tock, tock, tock." A tiny sound came from each of the eggs, and soon four new baby sparrows hatched in the cozy nest.

Then the Very Worried Sparrow... smiled!

"I can't wait to
see them grow," he said. "We'll
care for them and teach them to fly.
And I will tell them about God our
Father, who made the world and
everything in it, and who knows each sparrow. They won't have
to worry for a single day."

Then the Very Worried Sparrow flew up into the blue sky.

"Cheep, cheep," he sang, "cheep, cheep, cheep!" loudly
enough to burst with happiness.

*P*auline
BOOKS & MEDIA

The Daughters of St. Paul operate book and media centers at the following addresses. Visit, call or write the one nearest you today, or find us on the World Wide Web, www.pauline.org

CALIFORNIA
3908 Sepulveda Blvd, Culver City, CA 90230   310-397-8676
2460 Broadway Street, Redwood City, CA 94063   650-369-4230
5945 Balboa Avenue, San Diego, CA 92111   858-565-9181
FLORIDA
145 S.W. 107th Avenue, Miami, FL 33174   305-559-6715
HAWAII
1143 Bishop Street, Honolulu, HI 96813   808-521-2731
Neighbor Islands call: 866-521-2731
ILLINOIS
172 North Michigan Avenue, Chicago, IL 60601   312-346-4228
LOUISIANA
4403 Veterans Memorial Blvd, Metairie, LA 70006   504-887-7631
MASSACHUSETTS
885 Providence Hwy, Dedham, MA 02026   781-326-5385
MISSOURI
9804 Watson Road, St. Louis, MO 63126   314-965-3512
NEW JERSEY
561 U.S. Route 1, Wick Plaza, Edison, NJ 08817   732-572-1200
NEW YORK
150 East 52nd Street, New York, NY 10022   212-754-1110
PENNSYLVANIA
9171-A Roosevelt Blvd, Philadelphia, PA 19114   215-676-9494
SOUTH CAROLINA
243 King Street, Charleston, SC 29401   843-577-0175
TENNESSEE
4811 Poplar Avenue, Memphis, TN 38117   901-761-2987
TEXAS
114 Main Plaza, San Antonio, TX 78205   210-224-8101
VIRGINIA
1025 King Street, Alexandria, VA 22314   703-549-3806
CANADA
3022 Dufferin Street, Toronto, ON M6B 3T5   416-781-9131

¡También somos su fuente para libros,
videos y música en español!